The Hidden Gem

Written by Ja'Mecha McKinney   Illustrated by Sarah K. Turner

Halo
PUBLISHING
INTERNATIONAL

ISBN: 978-1-63765-087-5
LCCN: 2021914869

Halo Publishing International, LLC
www.halopublishing.com

Printed and bound in the United States of America

This book is dedicated to Jr, Jacoby, Eli, and all the hidden gems. Always remember that you are unique and that there is no one better to be than yourself.

Sunny days are made for football! That's what my brothers and I say.

Today after school, we're out in the yard to play.

We run, we throw, we tackle, and juke.

"Let's get this game started!" I yell to the group.

Down, set, hut, and away we go! Coby takes off running; I'm just too slow.

I jump to tackle, but he jukes instead.

I dive to the ground, getting grass on my head.

As I stand back up, I loudly ask, "Hey Coby! How did you get that fast?"

"It's a gift!" Coby says, proud as can be.

"Well, who gave it to you? You think they can give it to me?" I ask confusedly.

Coby laughs and says, "You have your own gift, just keep playing. You'll see!" and with that he takes off and runs towards the tree.

This gift of mine, I wonder what it could be.

I snap back into focus when Eli passes the ball to me.

Down, set, hut, and away we go! Headed for a touchdown, but I'm just too slow.

SMACK makes the sound as I'm knocked to the ground.

Tears begin to fall, and on my face there's a frown.

"You're hitting too hard, it's hurting me," I cry.

"I'm sorry, Jr, I didn't mean to. I must be getting stronger."

"Maybe strength is my gift!" he exclaims happily.

Before I can ask how he knows, Eli takes off running!

This gift of mine, I have to find it.

So I try everything!

Can I kick the ball really far? Nope.
Or jump really high? Nah.

Can I be as fast as Coby? No way.
Or as strong as Eli? Not possible.

I've run out of gifts and none were for me.

I tried and tried and it just won't be.

My gift must be hidden so well, that
even I can't see.

I run back into the house to think of more ideas, when my aunt Rose finds me.

"Why aren't you outside playing?" she asks.

"I'm trying to find my gift, but I've run out of ideas. Can you help me?"

"What gift?"

I sigh. "Eli and Coby both have gifts that make them special and really good at football. Eli is super strong and Coby can run really fast. I need to find my gift so that I can be good like them."

19

"Oh honey, you are already soooo special. You're a hidden gem." she says, as she comes to sit beside me.

"A hidden gem? What does that mean?"

"It means that your gift has been with you this entire time. There are many gifts one could have in football, whether it's a nice throw, super speed, or good blocks. But the best gift you can have in football is heart."

"Heart?" I ask, with a twisted face.

"Yes, heart. Having heart in football means you never give up; you keep trying and working to get better. Having heart will carry you through life. You're a gem, honey, precious and prized.

"Thanks, Auntie! You've found my gift! The best gift of all."

"So, now that you know your gift, what will you do with it?" she asks.

I'm going to use it! I know that I may not be the fastest runner, or have the strongest defense, but I will keep working hard and trying my best. I won't ever give up. I promise!

CPSIA information can be obtained
at www.ICGtesting.com
Printed in the USA
BVHW092304301121
622792BV00002B/33